For Arlo

First U.S. edition 2018

Library of Congress Catalog Card Number pending
ISBN 978-1-5362-0282-3

18 19 20 21 22 23 TWP 10 9 8 7 6 5 4 3 2 1

Printed in Johor Bahru, Malaysia

This book was typeset in Times New Roman.
The illustrations were done in ink and watercolor.

TEMPLAR BOOKS

an imprint of
Candlewick Press
99 Dover Street
Somerville, Massachusetts 02144
www.candlewick.com

Sam Usher

STORM

templar books
an imprint of Candlewick Press

When I woke up
this morning,
the wind was rattling
the windows.

I couldn't wait to
go outside.

I said, "Granddad! We could kick up the leaves,

swoop and fly,

and lean into the wind."

Granddad said, "It's the perfect day to fly the kite!
But we'll have to find it first."

Outside the wind blew and blew.

We looked for the kite in the cabinet.

I said, "Granddad, it's your cricket bat!
I remember this!"

And Granddad said,
"So do I!"

But we didn't find the kite.

The wind whooshed and whistled.

So we looked in the study.

And I said, "Remember when you let me
mail that important letter?"

Granddad said,
"Ah, yes, so I did.
We went by boat."

The wind gushed and howled.

But we still hadn't found the kite.
So we looked under the stairs and I said,
"Granddad, it's your telescope!
Do you remember our expedition?"

Granddad said, "Yes, we went into a secret cave,
and had a perfect picnic!"

We kept searching.
We thought we'd never
find the kite.

Then I shouted, "Granddad! Look!"

And Granddad said, "YES! You've found it!"

We were off to the park at last!

The kite flew so high.

Granddad said, "Hold on tight!"

We swooped
and flew.

But then I let go!

But Granddad
caught it.

He said,
"There's a storm brewing!
Let's head for home."

We prepared for landing.

Back at home,
Granddad said,
"The best adventure
is an adventure
shared."

And I agreed.

I hope it storms
again tomorrow.